THE MIGRATION OF DARKNESS

New and Selected Science Fiction Poems,
1975-2020

D1253076

THE MIGRATION OF DARKNESS

New and Selected Science Fiction Poems,
1975-2020

Poems by Peter Payack

Chthon Press/Assembly Line Studio

Chthon Press/Assembly Line Studio
Austin, Texas/Cambridge, Massachusetts

ISBN: 978-0-9824408-4-1

Cover art and book design by Peter Paul Payack
www.pppayack.com

This book is dedicated to

Rowan & Natalie

"Frequently consider the connection of all things in the universe ... We should not say 'I am an Athenian' or 'I am a Roman' but 'I am a citizen of the Universe.'"

–Marcus Aurelius, Meditations

"Know your place, in time and space."

–Peter Payack, The Book of Conceptual Anarchy, Vol. 1

THESE POEMS HAVE FIRST APPEARED IN THE FOLLOWING MAGAZINES AND NEWSPAPERS:

The New York Times:
Anti-Darwinism
The Dreams of Artificial Intelligence
Déja Boo
The Long & The Short Of It
Quantum Leap Frog
The Relationship of Roasted Chestnuts
1000 Angels
Perfect Marriage

The Paris Review:
The Average Person
Only Minutes
The Ultimate Party
The Babbling Fool

Rolling Stone:
Eggs & The Future
Stogie Sunset
Black Hole Limbo

The Cornell Review:
The Untimely Phone Call
The Result Of The Dig
The Beginning Of Things
The Light Of Human Reason
The Growth Of Human Ideas
Assembling The Model
Why I believe In Death

Asimov's Science Fiction:

Interstellar Dust

Moonburn

Why There Is Now

Wide Open Spaces

Cosmic Cowboys

Rainbow Bridges

The Migration Of Darkness

The Mover

The Mechanic

Star Web

Michelangelo and The Celestial Dome

Reflecting On Saturn

Moonlighting In The Daylight

The Moon And The Moth

Casting Glances

The Great Wall Of Wonder

A Trivial Matter

Soular

Anything Is Possible

Stellar Recycling

The Evolutionary Race

Timeless Graffiti

Scary, Scary Night

Surfing At Night

Do Not Despair

The Infinite Abyss

Dust

The Institute For Scientific, Non-rational Thought

Amazing/Fantastic Science Fiction Stories:
Timely Savings
A 250,000 Mile HighKu
Infinity
Spectacles For Spectacular Numbers
Microcosmos
Motion Denied
Quantum Couplets
Receding Galaxies
The Visionary Cosmographer

Creative Computing:
The Sun
A Brief Guide To The Theory of Relativity
Some Practical Uses of Black Holes
A (Very) Concise History of The Universe
Spinning Yarns
This Is The Way To The Stars
The Big Whoops Theory
The Evolution Of Death
Gentlemen's Watch

OTHER PUBLICATIONS:

Reader's Digest
The Village Voice
The Wall Street Journal
Pandora
Star-Line
Once Upon A Midnight
The Baffler
The Christian Science Monitor
Oink! (Paul Hoover, editor)
Mid-Atlantic Review (Billy Collins, editor)
Only Paper Today

TEXTBOOKS:

Knowing & Writing: New Perspectives on Classical Questions (Harper Collins)
Astronomy, From Earth To The Universe (Saunders College)
Envisioning Other Worlds: Science Fiction and Dystopia (Cornelsen, Berlin)

ANTHOLOGIES:

The Paris Review Anthology (Norton)
Asimov's Wonder of The World Anthology (Dial Press)
SKY ART, Sky Art Conference 2002, Delphi, Ikaria Greece. (M.I.T. Press)
Archaeoastronomy. (University of Maryland Press)
Le Scat Noir Encyclopaedia, (Black Skat Publications)
The Poets' Encyclopedia (Unmuzzled Ox)
The Umbral Anthology of Science Fiction Poetry
Burning with a Vision, Poetry of Science and the Fantastic (Owlswick Press)
Science Poetry
The Alchemy of Stars
The Best of Creative Computing, Volumes 1 & 2
Science Fiction Poetry

SKY ART:

As a Sky Artist, some of these poems were used in my Environmental
Poetry Projects at:

MIT's International Sky Art Conference
  at Cambridge 1981, 1986,
  at Delphi, Ikaria and Athens, Greece, 2002.
Ars Electronica, Linz, Austria, 1982
The Avant Garde Festival of New York
The Harvard University 350 Celebration
Boston's First Night
The Cambridge River Festival

The poem *No Free Will in Tomatoes* has been permanently sandblasted into the brick of the Davis Square Subway Station, on Boston's Red Line since 1984.

RHYSLING AWARD:

The poem *The Migration of Darkness* won the 1980 Rhysling Award for the Best Poem In Science fiction.

MANY OF THESE POEMS APPEARED IN THE FOLLOWING BOOKS AND CHAPBOOKS:

Cornucopia. New York Culture Review Press, New York City, NY. 1975
A Brief Guide To The Theory Of Relativity. Creative Computing, Morristown, NJ. 1977
The Evolution Of Death. Samisdat Press, Brigham, Quebec. 1977
Rainbow Bridges. Samisdat Press, San Jose CA. 1978
The Growth Of Human Ideas. Vehicle Press, Montreal, Canada. 1980
Stonehenge Unraveled. The Idea Works, Pequannock, NJ. 1981, 1992
Santa & The Ho Ho Ho Zone (with Paul JJ Payack). Chthon Press, Austin TX. 1994
No Free Will In Tomatoes. Zoland Books, Cambridge, MA, 1988
The Edible Anthology Of Poetry, Vol.1,2,3. Imaginary Press, Cambridge, MA. 1981-84
The Zen Of The Marathon (Centennial Edition). Marathon Sports, Cambridge, MA. 1996
Blanket Knowledge. Zoland Books, Cambridge, MA. 1997
The Zen Of America. The Imaginary Press, Cambridge, MA. 2002
Conceptual Anarchy, Selected Poems 1973-2009. Assembly Line Studios. 2009
On The River, The Cambridge Community Poem. Cambridge Arts Council. 2009
The Book Of Conceptual Anarchy, Vol. 1. Assembly Line Studios, Cambridge MA. 2012

THE MIGRATION OF DARKNESS

DUST

I had just finished mopping the dust into little piles
   in the various rooms of the house
when it dawned on me it was scattered heaps of cosmic dust,
   in many ways similar to those
that first aggregated into the stars, galaxies, and nebulae
which make up the substance of the universe.

As I was musing on the cosmic spark
   that set such a wondrous process into motion,
I realized I'd better stop stalling as it was almost dinner time.

To my utter astonishment
   when I re-entered the parlor,
the pile of dust was swirling in such a fantastic fashion
that the cobwebs condensed, glowed, and then burst into flame
in the form of a twinkling yellow sphere.

Sunstruck, I fled into the library
   only to find a miniature moon whirling
about the globe of Earth kept in the corner.
I then meekly ventured into the bedroom,
   when, with a sudden start, I took a flying leap
under the covers to avoid being struck by a streaking comet.

Later that night
   while still shuddering behind a pillow,
I peeked out and saw one of the most spectacular displays
   of shooting stars ever to be witnessed by humankind.
I suspect the comet had strayed into the parlor and broke up
while passing too close to the sun.

At long last,
    I looked upon all the work that was done
and was not done, and saw that it was good.

Tomorrow,
    I promised myself,
I'd clean up the mess with a vacuum.

THE ULTIMATE PARTY

All 74 billion people who once
inhabited the Earth are invited
to a party. The invitations state
8 p.m., and to my surprise give
my apartment as the place. The
dress is casual. They all arrive
within a couple of hours of each
other. But the party's a bomb.
There is very little food, no space,
and the various languages present
a communications problem. After
a while, tempers grow short and fights
break out. One in the kitchen is
unusually violent for a party and
a man is stabbed. He turns out to be
the first man. He dies. In turn
everyone else disappears in order
of birth, dating back almost three million
years. This takes some time, and goes
on well into the middle of the night.
Finally I am left alone with
74 billion cups and glasses to clean.
I put it off until morning.

STELLAR RECYCLING

I see a grocery bag
that has emblazoned
on it in large letters:
"I used to be
a plastic bottle."

And I think,
Ha! How narrow-minded!

Maybe I'll get a tattoo
on my forearm
that states:

"I used to be
the inside of a star."

And will be
once again.

THE BEGINNING OF THINGS

At the present time there are three theories concerning the paving over of the world. The first theory states that the Earth has always been and always will be paved, as pavement is continually created. This aesthetic theory allows the pavement to regenerate in perpetuum out of nothing. The second theory holds that the pavement (macadam, concrete, crushed stone, asphalt) comes and goes in cyclical fashion with periods when the surface of the Earth is more prone to paving than others. Some cite sunspot activity as the cause; others claim more ephemeral causal relationships. The third theory, and the one which receives the most ridicule, suggests that the surface of the Earth was not always paved, and at some time in the distant past there was no such thing as a paved surface. It goes so far as to postulate such fanciful notions as forest, field, and creature. As can be expected, this theory is held mostly by mystics, poets, and other misfits. This is where the matter rests at the present moment. The fact is that as far back as history is recorded the surface of the planet has always been paved, and as far as we can surmise, it always will be. Science offers no definitive answer to this most perplexing question.

THE MIGRATION OF DARKNESS

Each evening, shortly after sunset,
darkness covers the land.
    Having mystified thinkers for millennia,
    the mechanism for this occurrence
    has now been identified: migration.
Darkness, it has been found, is composed
of an almost infinite number of particles,
which roost and reproduce up north
where they have fewer natural enemies.
    forest fires, lampposts, lasers, blazing sunlight,
    torches, candles, lighthouses, limelight, and electricity
    are relatively rate in the polar regions.
These lightweight bits of darkness
flock together and fly south each evening
to more fertile land in a never-ending search
got an abundant food supply.
with the coming of the rising sun,
they return to their northern nesting grounds.
However, not all specks of darkness migrate.
Some that are less adventurous
    or downright lazy
choose to stay behind.
These covey together, in varying numbers,
seeking shelter from the strong sunlight
    by gathering under leafy trees, behind
    large rocks, and underneath umbrellas;
    hiding in alleys, between parked cars,
    in caves, and inside empty pockets.
These clusters are perceived by us as shadows.
They have a somewhat shorter life span
than those which migrate.

THE VISIONARY COSMOGRAPHER

Surveying the celestial spaces
with the aid of a kaleidoscope

∞

ANTIMATTER

Groundless speculation

SOME POSSIBLE EXPLANATIONS
FOR THE DISAPPEARANCE OF THE DINOSAURS

1. Like hula hoops, Edsels and polyester leisure suits, they are hopelessly out of date.

2. Stuck on the Long Island Expressway.

3. Want their share of the petroleum profits.

4. Waiting for the Red Sox to win the World Series before coming back. This could be the year!

5. Want Amnesty International to free imprisoned "Brothers" from museums around the world.

6. They are off the beaten path.

7. Upset at Noah for refusing to let them board "The Ark."

8. They want their likenesses on Mr. Rushmore.

9. Their number was up.

10. Had too many dinosaur eggs in one basket.

11. A callous cut of the cosmic cards.

12. Waiting for Godot.

13. Embarrassed to have turned into chickens.

ADVICE FROM THE MESOZOIC AGE

The dinosaurs didn't really do much
with their 200 million year reign of the planet
except run around and eat each other.

Don't be a dinosaur.

THE MOON & THE MOTH

The moth,
programmed by untold eons
    of evolution,
uses the moon as a beacon
to navigate its flight.

But how has the moon
fallen from the nighttime sky
    and become attached
to this post on the porch?

This white-winged lunar explorer
using all the bug logic
    at her dutiful disposal
frantically orbits the porch light
    like a crazed Apollo astronaut
on an endless excursion
to oblivion.

As a deus ex machina of sorts
in this little insect drama,
    I mercifully
switch off the light.

Now free
from the mesmerizing pull
    of the moon,
the moth breaks out of orbit
    and flutters
safely back to Earth.

On this flight
    at least,
the fates flew with her.

THE ORIGIN OF THE MATERIAL WORLD

Long before the Earth was formed
it was postulated that the nothingness
    which existed everywhere
    in the universe
could be condensed and compacted
into a state of fluid equilibrium.
In this way it would form the substratum
of the material world.

With the help of a primitive compression chamber,
small bits of nothingness
were first compacted into ideas
    however fleeting.
A person would get an idea
then immediately forget it.
Much head scratching was in evidence.

Sometime later
    though technically
    in an eternal world of nothingness
    time doesn't exist
the first idea was captured and stabilized.

The mechanical device to accomplish this feat
resembled a think tank
    with a vacuum cleaner attached
    to the end of the hose.
One by one these captured ideas
were transferred into a larger chamber.

Then the unanticipated happened.
The trapped ideas began mating with one another,
        and freak of nature that it was
their offspring were genetically mutated.
These biologically altered ideas
were born into the world as material objects:
        Planets, gardenias, books, manatees,
        gothic cathedrals, VCR's, mountains,
        hub caps and shoes, etc.
Things rained down from the sky
in a torrential downpour.
The world of nothingness melted away
like snow in a warm spring rain.

THE INFINITE ABYSS

Once mom died
I felt the weight and immensity
of *never* and *forever*.

BLANKET KNOWLEDGE

We walk under the shade of the only maple on the beach at Walden Pond when Susan, who is on an endless search for the perfect tan asks, "Where should I put the blanket. Which way is the Sun going?"

Being the wise guy that I am I say, "why this way." I wave my hand in a grand gesture across the sky and state, "the same way its been going for the last 4 and a half billion years!" That's when the debate started.

Susan insists that last week it went a different way, and she has the sunburn to prove it!

I say, somewhat professorially, "I am sorry about the sunburn and even more sorry to disagree, but the sun does rise in the east and set in the west, basic Earth Science 101.

"Duh!" she says.

"And that is east over there!" I say pointing.

To that she retorts, "that's just your opinion."

"Well," I reason out loud, "if you accept Heraclitus' idea that 'all things are in process and nothing stays the same,' I guess...." But that's not what Susan's thinking. She's thinking that I'm dead wrong and won't admit it.

I then take the approach that maybe Susan is referring to the time when the Earth's magnetic field reversed about 70,000 years ago.

But no. She's not. Not at all.

Maybe, I suggest, She's thinking about the statement in the Bible which asserts that the Sun stood still for a day. Susan glares and demands I spread the blanket where she wants it, then asks me to stop blocking her sun.

Where, I wonder, is Henry David Thoreau when you really need him?

ANYTHING IS POSSIBLE

If the Tyrannosaurus Rex
could change into a chicken,

As contemporary
evolutionary theory holds

Then
anything is possible,
I guess.

THE GREAT WALL OF WONDER

At the edge of the universe
   there runs a colossal curving wall
beyond which lies an unknowable nothing.

Envisioned as a defensive barrier
   against this alien void
the wall was begun in the time primeval,
   the first foundations being laid
shortly after the Big Bang.

It's a continuously expanded border
which resembles the Great Wall of China
   except that its length is measured in light years,
and it is made out of more ethereal materials
including moons, small planets, & asteroids,
   with solidified clouds of cosmic dust
used as celestial cement.

Lofty watchtowers
with blazing quasars positioned on top
   were erected at strategic intervals
along this monumental fortification,
   to stand on perpetual guard against
the ever-lurking legions of nothingness.

MICHELANGELO & THE CELESTIAL DOME

A wealthy patron of the arts petitioned Michelangelo
  to fresco the firmament
  of the nighttime sky
with "celestial and otherwise cosmic designs."

Up until that time,
  from the beginning of time,
the firmament had been black, stark and dark.
The knowledgeable opinion
was that the cosmos had been hurriedly constructed
  (in less than a week's time
  was the ongoing jest)
with the apparent emphasis on utility and function.
Decorating it, or any esthetic impulses for that matter,
was probably not included in the budgetary allowances.
And the contractor having a celestial dome to build
  with a limited expense account
was understandably hesitant to do any extra work,
  no matter how artistic,
that wasn't specifically spelled out in the contract.

Michelangelo was at first reluctant
  to accept such a colossal commission,
but was cajoled into taking it.
He responded with one of the world's "timeless" masterpieces
  bursting with immense power, scope, and vitality.

For this endeavor he constructed a towering scaffold
  upon which he could lie
and paint with the most realistic
  and minute detail.

The firmament as envisioned and portrayed by the artist
      is a huge living organism
with billions upon billions of heavenly objects
      majestically and poetically
positioned about the pitch-black dome.

Red giant stars, yellowish moons, planets inhabited by
      peculiar yet intriguing civilizations, galaxies and
      galactic clusters, ringed planets, comets with long
      hairy tails, nebulae, and shooting stars
are all depicted in a most compelling cosmic composition.

He even painted some stars in cunning configurations
      which cleverly suggest such earth objects
      as animals, people, and crafted items.
These designs have come to be known as "constellations."
Whether Michelangelo actually intended the stars
to be perceived in these patterns
      as direct representations
or whether they are unintended optical illusions
is a matter of much debate and speculation.

This part of the fresco,
      mainly painted directly overhead,
was completed after four years of back-breaking work.
Yet despite the artist's highly acclaimed accomplishment
      and much to Michelangelo's dismay
he was again called upon to enhance his masterpiece
as his patron demanded something more diverting,
amusing, unearthly, and unimaginable along the edges.

This time, however, much of Michelangelo's displeasure,
　　his violent changes in mood, and a sense of being
　　at odds with himself, his patron, and the universe
in general became vividly evident in his work.

His previously radiant vision darkened
to include such diabolical and depressing inventions
as an infinite universe forever expanding
　　into a cold frozen void of nothingness,
antimatter which annihilates matter upon contact,
exploding galaxies, lifeless bone-dry planets,
　　deadly cosmic rays, and black holes
which were depicted as swallowing up and obliterating
much of the masterpiece he had previously painted.

Michelangelo then climbed down from the scaffolding
and stepped back to inspect what his hand had rendered.
　　He paused to wonder wearily
if he would be called upon again to aggrandize his work
　　with evermore incredible inventions
to meet his patron's insatiable desire
for the fantastic and paradoxical.

DIRECTIONS

All roads lead to Rome and Sciarappa Street in Cambridge is no exception. I finally figured it out this afternoon on my way home from work:

Going north, turn left about two city blocks past the Renaissance. Drive about a mile (first you pass the Dark Ages on the right, and the Sacking of Europe by the Goths on the left). Then take a sharp right at the Beginning of the Christian Era. It's a really big intersection in history, and there's no way you can miss it. Two more miles and you're there!

Ironically enough, I missed the turn at 753 B.C. and was halfway back to the Stone Age before I discovered my mistake. It wasn't until almost midnight that I got home again.

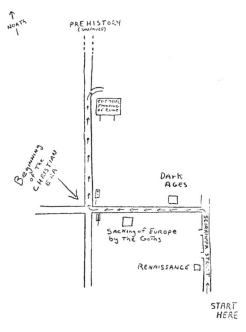

Hand drawing by Peter Payack, 1977

THE NIGHT THE HEAVENS FELL
-a childhood memory-

The night of the Perseid shower of shooting stars
we snuck out into the darkness minutes after midnight
    and gathered up as many of the fallen stars
as our greedy little hands could hold.

The yellow stars were the size of baseballs
    so we grabbed our gloves
and tried shagging them as they bounded out of the heavens.
Sure I made a few errors, but nobody was keeping score;
it was all in fun.

The red stars were as big as beachballs,
    and being bloated with gas,
floated rather than fell to earth.
We bounced them about until they either burst
or got caught on a high, out of reach, place.
We lost a couple in the cedar tree.

The miniature white stars
were too hot to touch even with a baseball mitt,
    so we let them drop to the ground.
Luckily, my father kept some golf clubs in the garage.
We used these to putt the little white balls
    into the black holes
we found scattered about the newly-mown lawn.
We couldn't miss sinking them.

The biggest challenge of the whole night
(if you don't count sneaking out of the house
    without waking my father)
was catching the comets, which were whizzing overhead,
    onto the end of a long stick.
Once hooked, they would spin around like sparkling pinwheels
    until their energy was spent;
the icy comets would plop to the ground
with slushy thuds.

We stored the comets in an ice cooler until we had enough
    (it took us almost until dawn).
Then we had the best snowball fight I can ever remember!
Maybe, because it was in August.

STELLABRELLA

An umbrella
for a shower of shooting
stars
!

∞

BLACK HOLE LIMBO

the infinite
collapses
the
imper
cep
ti
ble

.

ASSEMBLING THE MODEL

A standard model of reality comes to me in the mail. At $4.95 I feel
it's quite a bargain. Actually since it's very intricate and made to scale,
the kit is worth much more than the money I paid for it. There are
three separate bags of different color plastics with an 800-page manual
for assembly. The first bag I open is filled with 100 billion galaxies.
A small note explains that each galaxy is composed of 100 billion
individual stars, an unheard of number of planets, asteroids, and other
manifestations of astronomical paraphernalia. Five little jars of paint
are supplied with a tiny camel's hair brush to make the stars accurate
in appearance. The second bag is filled with philosophical abstracts:
Hegelian absolutes, Platonic nouses, and Heisenbergian uncertainties,
along with countless thousands of minor conceptions. Some of these
are particularly hard for the lay person to grasp, so miniature tweezers
are supplied. The third package contains assorted manifestations of
things in general: minerals, gravity, human beings, light, artifacts of
unknown civilizations, animals, oceans, doubts, food stuffs,
inspirations, et cetera. An itemized list, along with a magnifying glass,
is included inside the package. I'm very pleased with the model and
have it spread throughout the house, ready for assembly. It's not until
then that I notice the fine print: "The price of the standard model does
not include a tube of glue. The deluxe model of reality ($5.25) contains
both a tube of glue and decals."

PROTOZOAN PRIDE

I like
the thought
that I am an animal
with 1.7 billion years
of evolution behind me.

It gives me
a past I can be proud of.

∞

ALIEN INVASION

These words are now inside your head.

THE MOON OUT OF TUNE

At 9:30 in the morning
the moon is still
lingering around
like a drunken party guest
who doesn't know
when to leave.

"Get out of here
you partied out orb.
The planets and stars
were up all night too
but split at sunrise.
Take the cue!"

It just
stares off listening,
with a stone cold look
on its bleached out
pocked marked face

obviously
"hung over."

THE MECHANIC

The cosmic mechanic is an old-fashioned guy
    whose reputation has grown
to all ends of the mechanistic universe.
In addition to standard jobs
    like mufflers, brakes, and shocks,
his expertise includes:
greasing-up spiral galaxies
    to keep them rotating friction free;
tuning-up stars
    to minimize misfiring solar flares
    and eliminate backfiring sun spots;
and balancing & aligning solar systems
    (it's surprising how one unbalanced planet
    can throw a whole system out of whack).
No ordinary grease monkey is he!

And he's honest, too.
You can trust his personal judgment
as to whether an abused planet
that has been "run to the ground"
    needs a complete overhaul,
or if it is simply time to "junk it,"
and invest in a newer model.
He is currently mulling over the fate of Earth.

To show you what a traditionalist he is,
he still provides complete road service
    for a very old fashioned price.

His most common call for help,
	as you might suspect,
is to come to the aid of crippled comets
which have carelessly wandered too close to the sun.
Most often they have been completely "totaled"
and are unable to move under their own power.
He'll tell it to you straight,
	and then tow the burnt out cinder
to the edge of the observable universe
and push the "heap" over the ultimate edge.

Being a civic minded individual,
	he has erected
(with money out of his own pocket, no less)
a white picket fence on the border of the universe
so that passerbys won't be appalled
	by the discarded wrecks
of planets, stars and galaxies;
Their ruined remains rusting and rotting
unceremoniously for all eternity.

Still somewhat of a diehard
	in the field of traditional mechanics,
he won't touch black holes, pulsars or quasars.
He doesn't like to handle these
	"new fangled foreign jobs."
These he leaves in the hands of the younger generation
of newly trained "quantum mechanics"
with their recalibrated tools,
computerized tune-ups,
and relative view of things.

A BRIEF GUIDE TO
THE THEORY OF RELATIVITY
(in easy-to-understand language)

When the theory of relativity was first propagated by Albert Einstein in 1905, it was said that only twelve men could understand it. Unfortunately that was 115 years ago. And they are probably all dead now. So we cannot look to them for help, but must rely on our own resources.

A short time ago it came to me in dream or vision or television commercial (I can't remember which) to use the metaphor of a train when describing the mechanics of relativity. The Long Island Railroad is the perfect example.

One of the paradoxes of relativity is that of time. Picture yourself on a Long Island Railroad commuter train at rush hour. There is a clock on the station wall, and further suppose that it works. Remember a vivid imagination is important. The clock on the wall says 5:00 when the train pulls out at the speed of light. After a second the train has traveled 186,000 miles, or past Hempstead anyway. To the people on the train it will seem as if one second has passed, and yet if they look back at the clock on the station wall, it still says 5:00. Time on the train has come to a stop! At first glance it may seem that we are dealing with a purely logical contradiction.

But certainly this is not so for anyone who has ever ridden on the Long Island Railroad, where time always seems stopped.

This conclusively proves that there is no universal time, and even though it might seem so to some New Yorkers, the universe does not run on Eastern Standard Time.

Another paradox we are confronted with is the length contradiction. Some say that John Dillinger had the longest one at 18 inches, and that the proof is in the Smithsonian.

Personally, I doubt this claim. Nevertheless, when we continue our train ride at the speed of light, hopefully avoiding all delays, we would find some amazing changes in appearances as we pass through stations along the way. People in the stations will think that the train has become shorter while to us in the train it will appear that the platforms are thinner and taller. This is not unusual right after cocktails. The only person things won't seem distorted to is John Dillinger, and that's because he's dead. To a dead person, length, width and even relativity don't matter much.

In a straightforward manner, then, the theory of relativity provides us with a most dizzying picture of the world about us. Unfortunately for us on this train, technology has not increased as rapidly as theory, and no brakes were provided for stopping a train at 186,000 miles per second.

SOME PRACTICAL USES
OF BLACK HOLES

"A black hole's gravitational field is so intense that anything that approaches it is trapped; nothing can escape its grasp."

a. *Prevent Jailbreaks.* Locate black holes in prison yards to prevent escapes. They can be situated in schools for the same purpose.

b. *Develop a Magnetic Personality.* For the man who wants to attract women, place one in the breast pocket of your debonair sportscoat. It can be scented to smell like aftershave if desired.

c. *Mouse Traps.* Replace costly Swiss cheese with black holes.

d. *Eliminate Lost Thoughts.* Have a reputable surgeon implant a black hole between your ears so that no ingenious thoughts will escape you.

e. *Household Rubbish Disposals.* Hire a plumber to install a black hole in your kitchen, next to the sink.

f. *Attention Getters.* A clown who wants to captivate a crowd should insert a black hole in his red rubber nose.

g. *Insect Controllers.* Have a black hole flattened by a black-(hole)-smith so that it is paper thin, and use it as flypaper. Caution: Do not place in areas frequented by children and small pets.

h. *Bait.* Use to bait fishhooks.

1. *Advertising.* Insert a black hole in magazine ads to snare new subscribers.

INFINITE LOVE

Falling for a black hole.

$$\infty$$

INTERSTELLAR DUST

Raison d'etre
for the vacuum of space.

OPERATION SKYMINE

A complex and highly technological mining technique has been developed to meet the recent demand for organic and natural colors. Operation Skymine, as the process is known, utilizes a highly mobile floating mechanism that in many respects resembles a deep sea oil-drilling platform, only inversely so. Instead of sinking drills deep into the bedrock, the equipment floats in clouds and scoops up the spectacular colors of the sky with a giant gossamer shovel-like device. The floating platform is a full working factory, which harvests these natural colors, separates them according to spectral analysis, deepfreezes them to preserve their brilliance, and packages them for distribution, all in a single stroke.

Whereas the majority of orders come for the resplendent colors of the rainbow, it is more likely to see these floating processors glimmering high in the late afternoon sunshine. They trail after the towering thunderheads of the immense summertime squall lines, mining the rainbows before they fade into commercial worthlessness.

It takes a certain type of rugged individual to do this seasonal and back-breaking work. A hardworking experienced crew can usually dismantle an entire rainbow without much waste in less than a half hour. In the Wintertime when rainbows are less frequent, exploratory teams usually head northward and await the onset of the aurora borealis. "That's where the real money is," explains the cigar-chomping foreman of one of the most legendary expeditionary teams. "This chilly and challenging frontier is where the skill of the crew comes in," he continued, but he also acknowledged that with the unpredictability of the northern lights it is more a matter of being in the right place at the right time.

The mining of less dramatic dawns and sunsets is left for the off-season, and only then if the money gets tight. "Unless you hit a really brilliant one, which nowadays occurs only rarely, it's hardly worth the time, expense. and effort," he says. These are usually used as training runs for apprentices, or left for the amateur hobbyists with their home-built contraptions, trying to make a few extra bucks.

ONLY MINUTES

It would take
an infinite number
of monkeys,
an infinite amount
of time to write
this poem using
typewriters and
random chance.

For instance,
it would take 10,000
monkeys 150 years
to achieve one "it would."

As it was,
it took this ponderous poet
only minutes.

SUNBLOCK 5 BILLION

Here's something to be nostalgic about: A stinging sunburn!
I remember going to the Jersey Shore, playing in the sun all day and
burning to the point where you would make a lobster look anemic.
Later at night while driving home on the jammed Garden State
Parkway, with the windows rolled down, you would hear a collective
moan from every car within earshot as they played the commercial on
WABC for relief of SUNBURN! Ah, for the good 'ol days! And you
think computers and VCR's represent the biggest changes of the last
quarter century.

Ha! Well, in the enlightened nineties, nobody goes to the beach
without a sun block. A few years ago, you could get protection from
the sun with a block numbered, say, 5, which would allow to ample
protection. Well, this is America, and that wasn't good enough. So
last year Monica asked me to buy sunblock with a protection of 20.
As she would only stay at the beach for less than an hour, that seemed
reasonable enough. This year, with weekly newspaper accounts of the
widening hole in the Ozone layer over Antarctica, I was assigned to
find her a sun block of 35. From what I understand, you could lie naked
in the sunlight, on a mountain top at the Equator, for the better part of
your adult life and still not burn. Even though she douses herself with
this, she now only goes to the beach after 4 PM on rainy days.

Then, I suggested an Idea to her: "How about Sunblock 5 Billion?"
This would not only be effective under normal beach conditions, but
would also work in case the Sun goes Supernova while vacationing
on Cape Cod. She like the idea. Except she advised me against using
PABA in the formula. She fears her sensitive skin might prove allergic
to it.

PICK YOUR (INTERPLANETARY) POISON

I know you hate the short winter nights

and cold temperatures.
But that is what gives us
the long, warm summer days.

After all, we live on a planet
with a tilted axis.

Try to find pleasure in both.

Perhaps a solution would be
to rocket to planet without a tilted axis,
like Venus.

But then Venus has an air temperature
of 900 degrees
and an atmosphere of carbon dioxide.

Talk about a bad hair day!

CONCEPTUALIZING TIME

Tomorrow is a concept
that can only exist on a planet
which rotates on its axis
as it revolves around a star.

Likewise with years, days,
minutes and seconds.

Infinity and eternity
are two sides to the same coin.
Although in the infinite
and eternal universe,
a coin doesn't really make sense.
Maybe a mobius strip,
but not a coin.

Money representing
units of work
doesn't count for much either.

Take it or leave it.
It's just my two cents worth.

THE HOODLUM SHADOWS

Turning the clocks back
I forgot to reset the shadows.

So the shadows ran
an hour behind
all day long.

Once the sun went down
the shadows stood around
an extra hour,
loitering
like hoodlums on a street corner.

A shadow in the dark
looks like the negative
of a picture.

I called the cops
on the hoodlum shadows
for disturbing my peace of mind
with their shady shenanigans
and wicked wisecracks.

By the time the cops
finally arrived,
the shadows had slipped away
into the darkness
like night falling
on the dark side of the moon.

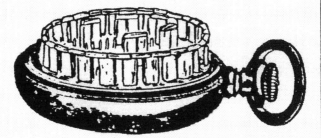

Original Collage of The Stonehenge Watch circa 1978

THE SUN
-A Play-

Instructions: Build a stage in the middle of an open field. Have the audience seated on this stage. Have plenty of refreshments available.

Act I
THE SUN: The Sun rises with a show of spectacular colors and pageantry.
OPTIONAL: (clouds may be used to heighten the effect, along with chirping birds.)
THE AUDIENCE: Bursts into applause, with oohs and aahs interspersed.

Intermission (approximately 6 1/2 hours)

Act II
THE SUN: The sun reaches the highest point in the sky.
THE AUDIENCE: Cheers and claps, but with some catcalls intermixed in anticipation of the sun's imminent descent.
(NOTE: if stage is located at the equator, wild cheering in appreciation of the extra effort.)

Intermission (approximately 6 1/2 hours)

Act III
THE SUN: The sun sets below the Earth's horizon-very colorful, but more austere and formal than in Act I.
THE AUDIENCE: A foreboding atmosphere prevails, as the audience claps in both appreciation and relief. As the sun begins to disappear the audience grows tense. Two or three people faint when the finality of the act becomes apparent. Some demand their money back.

Just before the curtain of darkness falls, a plane flies overhead and skywrites in large white letters:

THE END....

FOSSILIZED ETHEREAL PHENOMENA

Archeologists have unearthed and verified
    the startling discovery
of a number of petrified, calcified & fossilized
    moonbeams, shadows, rainbows,
halos & thunderbolts.

A truant New Jersey Schoolboy
    who literally "stumbled" over the fossils
is credited with the find.
After a driving rainstorm he was playing
    under a busy overpass
when he tripped on what appeared to be a hub cap.

Upon closer examination by his parole officer
    it was found to be
a partially exposed petrified thunderbolt.
Subsequent investigation by archeologists
found the area teeming,
    not only with discarded car parts,
but also with fossilized ethereal phenomenon.

The thunderbolts, rainbows & shadows
    all found in the upper layers of earth
are a relatively recent 10,000 years old.
While the halos and moonbeams
    date back to almost a million years,
and are exceedingly brittle.

Scientists are speculating as to their origins.
    Whether they occur "naturally"
or are early human artifacts
has yet to be determined.

One theory is that when early humans happened upon
    a rainbow or a moonbeam
they would gather it up quickly,
    before it vaporized into nothingness,
and carry it back to the campsite.
There a craftsman would preserve it,
    with a lost process,
and forge it into colorful rings, bracelets, necklaces
and other ornaments.

Today you can frequently find New Jersey truants
    slyly hawking these hot items
on Madison Ave. in Manhattan.

QUANTUM COUPLET

The sex life of a quark,
at best, a momentary spark!

∞

TRUE LUST

My hormones
are in love with your hormones.

∞

PERFECT MARRIAGE

An archeologist & a grave digger.

THE BABBLING FOOL

An ancient Babylonian, lost in the
pages of unwritten history books, was
talking with the foreman of a local
construction company. They were discussing
the transportation of ceramic bricks back
to the 4th millennium B.C. for use in
the construction of the Tower of Babel.
However, after a little more than an hour,
the negotiations fell through.
Obviously frustrated, after sending the
Babylonian back almost 6,000 years with one
swift kick, the foreman said to me:
"The man drove a hard bargain, and
the price was right. But I just couldn't
carry out a business deal with a grown man
who babbled so. Made me feel like
the guy had his head up his ancient ass."

COMPUTER VISION

Binary spots before your eyes.

∞

TIME

The *zen* of *when*

IT IS TOO HOT

"It is too hot
to live," said
the dead man.

"It is too hot
to be dead," said
the living man.

"It is too hot, let us
not argue," said
the mute man.

"Yes indeed, it is too hot
to waste words on one
another," said the deaf man.

"It is too hot
to write," I said.

"It is too hot
to read the nonsense
you write," she said.

"Fuck you," I said.

"It is too hot," she said.

INFINITY

****
****
****
****
****
****
****
****
****
****
****
****
****
****
****
****
****
****
****
****
****
****
****
****
****
****
****
****
****
****
****
***, et cetera.

THE BARREL & BEYOND

The philosophical pickle ponders both that which is and that which might be beyond The Barrel, as speculative thought is usually described. He wonders what makes a cucumber pickled, and speculates whether life as we know it exists in the Beyond. After many months of study he determines that reality is made up of four primary elements: cucumbers, brine, pickling spices, and The Barrel. Further he concludes that there exists a Prime Mover who not only sets the whole works in motion, but also decides what is to be, gives order to The Barrel and Beyond, and generally operates outside the limits of normal pickle thought and morality. That night, at dinner time, the Prime Mover eats the philosophical pickle with a hamburger.

SURFING AT NIGHT

I had a dream
in which I'm floating
in the ocean,
on a bed of blue-green algae.

There was algae as far as I could see,
and I heard a voice say,

"The difference
between living and dying,
being and non-being,
is just where you catch the wave."

I covered my head
with my blanket
and rode the wave back to sleep.

A (VERY)
CONCISE HISTORY
OF THE UNIVERSE

Sissssssssssss.   BOOM!   Entropic Doom.

∞

ANTI-DARWINISM

Survival of the *Nitwittiest*.

1000 ANGELS
-revisited-

In the Middle Ages
the Scholastic Philosophers
argued hair-splitting points
which today are deemed,
rather silly and pointless,

like how many
angels could stand
on the head of a pin.

Today,
some scientists
believe that
all the matter of
the yet to be born universe
was encapsulated
in a space
less then the size
of an atomic particle

Where the temperature
was over 1500 billion degrees
and conditions extremely chaotic.

And I think,
how many angels
could stand inside
an atomic particle
withstanding temperatures
in excess billions of degrees
in extremely chaotic conditions?

Where is St. Thomas Aquinas
when we really need him?

THE ONLY THING
YOU'LL NEED TO KNOW
ABOUT THE SUN
GOING SUPERNOVA

It would take
eight minutes
for us on Earth to realize
that the Sun has undergone
an untimely gravitational collapse
resulting in a catastrophic nuclear explosion
of light, heat, and charged particles
that would soon encapsulate the Earth,
boil off the oceans,
and fry us like clams.

In fact,
it might have happened
7 minutes
and 59 seconds ago....

THE ETERNAL OPTIMIST

Still waiting for the Comet Kohoutek.

∞

GOOGOL GOGGLES

Spectacles for spectacular numbers.

COPYING A COSMOS

I

On a piece of paper draw a picture of a star.
    Color it yellow.
Then draw four other stars of varying sizes
on four additional sheets of paper.
Make one extra large using the limits of the page.
    Color it red.
The smallest one will be a neutron star,
    use a black crayon on it.
The other two should be orange and blue-white.
Bring these to an instant copy center
and have them run off 40 billion copies of each picture
    using paper of the appropriate color.
Don't worry about the price;
The rate drops after the first 10,000 copies.
The colored paper is extra.

II

While these are being processed
draw some planets on other sheets of paper.
Include
    large planets, planets with rings,
    tiny crater-strewn planets, dead planets,
    planets with colorful bands of gas,
    planets inhabited by superior civilizations,
    and half-formed planets (planetoids).
When the copy center is finished duplicating
    the 200 billion stars,
bring them the planets.
They'll love you!
Since it is not known how many stars have planets
    100 million copies of each drawing should do it.

III

Get a really sharp pencil
and make random dots all over a sheet of white paper.
These dots will be the numberless atoms of hydrogen
 which flow randomly throughout interstellar space.
Try to make 100,000 on a page.
 If necessary use a microscope.
Make a trillion copies.
Technically this is not nearly enough hydrogen atoms
 but we have to draw the line somewhere.
Bring this load to a second printer.

IV

Next get a piece of pitch-black paper
 and have its blackness duplicated.
Have the attendant at a third duplicating center
 set the dial at infinity.
Tell him money is not object.
If you must, intimate that your
 "old man is really loaded!"
These black pages are the abysmal expanses
 of cold emptiness
 which most of galactic space consists of.
Place them in a freezer until ready for use.

V

Rent a fleet of 18-wheelers
 to transport the copies home.
Unload them in your front yard.
When this is accomplished you are almost finished.
Take a brief rest.

VI

Hand-letter invitations
and invite the whole neighborhood to a party
    to help with the completion of the project.
Threaten them by saying it's the only way
    you'll ever get the yard cleaned-up.
They'll come running!

VII

Ask the Fire Department to donate the services
    of their longest ladders.

VIII

On a clear windless night,
extend the ladders upward so that the tips
are resting against the rafters
    which keep the night sky from collapsing.
Anchor the ladders securely into terra firma:
Why risk a lawsuit from a careless neighbor?

IX

Using paste, tacks, staples, tape, and hooks
affix the copies to the underside of the celestial dome.
    Watch our for orbiting satellites!
Stars can be attached
        singly,
        put in pairs,
        grouped in clusters,
        or arranged in constellations.

Planets should be strewn around the individual stars.
The black pages of empty space
    should be taken out of the freezer
and along with the reprints of the hydrogen atoms,
    liberally affixed throughout.

X
If everyone co-operates,
    and nobody falls off a ladder,
the project should be completed by sunrise.

THE SEARCH FOR REALITY
- Updated (2020)-

Socrates,
the ancient Athenian gadfly,
who today
might have been put on Ritalin,
was the first to ask
the fundamental questions
of philosophy
which became the bedrock
of western civilization

What is truth?
What is goodness?
What is the place of humans in the universe?

Today,
the postmodern heirs to Socrates
carry on this self-reflective nature
although the questions
have changed:

How much does that cost?
What channel is that on?
Are those fake or real?

METAPHYSICIAN ON CALL?

I am amazed that I can fit
the whole Universe,
into my head,
as I meditate before
falling asleep.

I think of the 100 billion galaxies
    each made up of a 100 billion stars
and the endless, almost bizarre, assortment
of universal fireworks including
    quasars, black holes, shooting stars,
    dark energy, comets, cosmic rays,
    supernovas, meteor showers,
    magnetic storms, exploding galaxies
and the Big Bang.

All this cosmic ruckus
gives me a headache.

I take two aspirin,
and resolve to call
a metaphysician
in the morning.

SPINNING YARNS
RELATIVELY SPEAKING
a pinwheel poem

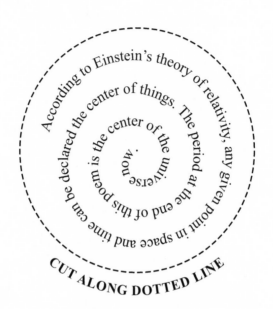

According to Einstein's theory of relativity, any given point in space and time can be declared the center of things. The period at the end of this poem is the center of the universe. now.

CUT ALONG DOTTED LINE

Instructions:

1. Copy page
2. Cut out along dotted line.
3. Place a pin through the period in the center of the poem, and then stick it into the eraser of a pencil.
4. Spin while reading

PHILOSOPHICAL EVOLUTION

Two Neanderthals debate the nature of the evolving brain. Its decreasing volume, as opposed to its ever increasing and deepening convolutions are analyzed & argued, as if the fate of Neanderthal civilization depended on it. All this takes place somewhere in Western Europe, most likely from the heavy tone of the discussion, in Germany. This in a sense is the beginning of the German philosophical tradition. Kant, Hegel, Schopenhauer and Nietzsche all in some way owe a debt to these early humans. Especially Nietzsche, with his deep-sunk eye sockets and his heavy brow.

THE INFINITY OF DIVINITY

If there is
an infinite number of universes

as contemporary
cosmology holds

then there must be
an infinite number of gods.

It would be
greedy for one god
to reign over
more than a single universe.

And greed is one
of the seven deadly sins.

No offense intended:
This is just the opinion
of a one-puny-planet poet.

I certainly don't need
the wrath of millions of billions
of gods on my head.

So, for Christ's
(Buddah's, Isis,' Apollo's, Shiva's,
Zoroaster's, Aphrodite's, Allah's,
Sheela na Gig's, Gaia's, Thor's,
Hera's, YHWH's, Tzazolteotl's, Jove's,
Manu's, Ēl's, Ishtar's, Ix Chel's, Inanna's,
Dionysus,' Ba'al's, Talapas' and God's)
sake,
back off!

THE BIG WHOOPS!
A Cosmocomical Theory of Creation

Since earliest human times, one of the great unsolved mysteries is the nature and origin of the universe. Now, scientists have put forward a bold new theory which elucidates not only the intricate web of the cosmic-evolutionary scenario but also gives meaning to the enigmatic happenings of everyday life. It links together through computer-aided mathematical models, such seemingly unrelated phenomena as black holes and holes in Swiss cheese, gravity, condominium and energy conversion, death, the theory of evolution and the birth of Richard Nixon, quasars, and why both half-baked cakes and fully baked civilizations fall.

The "BIG WHOOPS!" theory, as this daring new cosmological conception is called, contends that every object in the universe has a built-in whoops! factor that leads to its eventual downfall in an incongruous, if not downright silly, way.

According to the theory, this is an inherent component of reality's basic nature which can not be altered in any way. It explains why, when things seem to be going along smoothly, whoops! something happens that messes everything up. Say, an almost inconceivable giant red star, some 500 million kilometers in diameter, farcically collapses into a tiny white dwarf, not more than 20 kilometers across. Or, you are on your way to a close friend's funeral when you slip on a banana peel and rip your meticulously pressed pants. That's the whoops! factor at work.

Further, it is postulated that the more massive the material object, the larger and sillier is its potential whoops! Therefore, if we were to extrapolate back some 14 billion years to a time when all the matter of the universe was concentrated into a highly compressed primordial globule, you can readily see that it exploded and formed today's observable cosmos because of the whoops! factor at its absolute best!

This cosmocomical event can best be visualized by picturing in your mind this preposterous primeval atom as a cosmogonical whoopee cushion which is being blown-up for a party gag. After it has been properly inflated and placed on a chair (preferably under a pillow) one of the unsuspecting guests "sits on it," and in a manner of speaking lets the air out of the archetypal bag! Only in this singular case the air happens to be loaded with galaxies, pulsars, planets, stars, nebulae, comets, black holes, meteors, quarks and quasars that go hurling into all directions of space, and the universe is brought into being. Who blew it up, and who or what "sat on it" has not been addressed by these scientists who feel that these questions should be left to the realm of philosophical and theological inquiry.

The observations that led to the theoretical foundations of this theory were done at the Mt. Maldermer Observatory, in California, with the aid of its newly constructed 250-inch kaleidoscope.

DO NOT DESPAIR

If you ever
feel directionless,
remember that every hour
brings us 43,000 miles
closer to Globular Cluster M13
in the constellation Hercules.

Talk about goal orientation!

∞

MOTION DENIED

Why does inanimate object?

CITY OF SHADOWS

An ancient city, constructed entirely of shadows has been unearthed in an outlying district of Rome. This city has long been alluded to in ancient mythological and literary sources, but until now concrete proof of its existence has been unsubstantiated.

The first hints of the city's actuality came when a crew of ditch diggers struck an apparently empty cavity which resembled, in dimension and layout, a wine shop from antiquity. Consequent archeological investigation found it not to be an immaterial void but, rather, a well-founded building constructed of shadows.

Further excavations found the City of Shadows to be virtually intact. Scholars attribute its survival to the ingenious integration of experimental shadow construction with the established architectural techniques of columns, arches, and domes.

A high grade of shadow had to be utilized to withstand the onslaught of both the barbarians and time. The darkness needed to fabricate this quality of shadow was either mined by slaves from rich deposits in local caves, or gathered by street urchins on moonless winter nights. The darkness was then set into molds and baked in the sunlight, forming brick-like components.

It is now virtually certain that the Romans, who were engineering geniuses, borrowed this grandiose concept of building with shadows from the Greeks and, in particular, from Plato's allegorical Cave of Shadows. The Romans, who grasped little of metaphysical speculation, mistakenly interpreted Plato's philosophical dissertation as an architectural blueprint.

THE NECTAR OF THE GODS?

The water we drink
is the same that Dionysus,
Buddha and Jesus drank.

And the same
that the dinosaurs did, too.

Ditto for the air we breathe.

WATER,

From Shores of Walden Pond to the Edge of the Universe

(In Three Parts)

(1)

I go to Walden Pond,
and feel the water is special,
curative, restorative,
like some feel about the water at Lourdes
or the Ganges in India.

Of course it is not.
Its essence is no different
from the water in any other stream,
the ocean at Revere Beach
or even the toilet bowl.

But it is ok to feel the water is unique.
I do.
In an odd way it makes me feel happy.

It is ok to be happy,
even for an unfounded reason.

It's ok to feel sad.
The important thing is "to be."

The important thing is "to being."

Shakespeare probably
had this same idea,
but undoubtedly got a migraine over it.

I know I do!

(2)
We imbue meaning
to most things in life,
and it is no different
with purely physical objects
like water.

Even so,
I like to drink water
imported from Italy
since my ancestral relatives
come from Italy.

But my ancestral roots
probably go back to the Greeks
since Naples
was founded as the Greek Colony,
Neopolis, in the 4th century BC.

And before the Human Diaspora,
we all came from the ancient
savannahs of Africa.
Our ancestry
further goes back to the first mammals
all the way to the one-cell organisms,
amino acids
and nucleotides that floated about
in the primitive Earth's briny seas
billions of years ago,

to the coalescing elements
that were blasted out
of some unknown star.

I mean, in all this randomness,
who knew that one day I, a sentient
and self-reflective being,
would be sitting here
writing such foolishness?

But I still enjoy drinking spring water
imported from Italy
on the shores of Walden Pond.
No matter how inane.

(3)
Imposed meaning or not,
water is the blood of the Earth.

It flows through the arteries
of the planet in the rivers and streams,
pipelines, and it's ever
pulsating oceans and seas.

Water is in every living thing.

It binds us together
with people, animals
and plants alike.

DNA is the same throughout all life,
It's the sequence and number
that make humans different than a tomato.

NO FREE WILL IN TOMATOES

I place a tomato
on the windowsill
to ripen.

Slowly it turns red.

∞

MONKEY BUSINESS

Humans share 98.8 percent
of our DNA with chimpanzees
while surprisingly sharing 40%
of our DNA with tomatoes.

THE EVOLUTION OF DEATH

Death

first evolved
on Earth
two billion years ago
in the warm shallow seas.

All later advanced forms
evolved from these modest
slime-like beginnings.

The evolution of death
culminates with
the appearance of people,
where death is self-realized.

There is every reason to believe
that highly developed forms of death
also evolved
on other planets throughout our galaxy.

THE FABRIC OF SPACE

I go into the closet
and pull out my old nightshirt.
Black and full of holes,
I hold it up over my head
and am surprised to find
these holes resemble the stars of the night sky.
I find the constellations Virgo, Orion, and Leo.

There is something paradoxical
about the feel of the fabric.
The areas where there are holes are hot,
while the dark areas are cold
like the deep reaches of interstellar space.
Suddenly, the shirt seems to shrink
before my very eyes!

It is now clear to me
that what I first thought
was a giant moth hole in the middle
is actually a Black Hole
-that theoretical celestial void.
The stars slowly start to move
in a swirling fashion
resembling a galactic spiral.

I drop the nightshirt
as it starts to spin like a fiery pinwheel
on the Fourth of July.
Imploding upon itself
without even so much as a pop,
a nebulous whiff of smoke is
sucked into nothingness.

I'm a little hesitant
about picking out another shirt.

RELATIVITY REVISITED

Time only moves
in one direction

Except
in your head

∞

RECEDING GALAXIES

The Universe shows its age.

∞

TEXAS

This sentence is the universe,
with the words galaxies,
the letters stellar systems,
the commas quasars,
and the period a lone star.

ECHOES OF THE PAST

Backpacking through the tranquil Maine Woods, my buddies & I stumbled upon something you don't meet up with everyday, an "Echo Lake." When I yodeled a simple "hello" to test it out, you can well imagine how surprised we were to find that this rustic country lake was not only well-educated, but also pretentious enough to show it. It seemed to have taken at least a college level etymology course, because my boisterous salutation ricocheted back first as the Elizabethan "halloa," then the "hallow" of Middle English, followed by the Old French "hallo!" Maybe it attended Harvard Graduate School on a fellowship, because nothing could stop it now. It was as if the echo had been held captive deep in the lake's memory for eons and was only now surfacing and looking for an opportunity to demonstrate its erudition. As the sun started to set, Echo Lake continued reverberating with dimmer yet still decipherable tongues and etymologies passing back through Vulgar Latin, Italic, and even Indo-European variants. This could have been Echo Lake's doctoral defense, so we stood there restlessly, yet respectfully, like a bunch of critical college professors. Throughout that night, even with our heads buried deep in our sleeping bags, we could still hear Neanderthal, Cro-Magnum and Australopithecine phonemes rippling back and forth through the serene stillness. Finally, in the predawn mist, Echo Lake hesitated, yawned, and breathlessly gasped a series of almost inaudible and unintelligible primeval grunts and groans. It only took me and my colleagues a few minutes to groggily confer with one another and award it a "B+" ("A" for effort). After all that, we continued on our hike, carefully lifting our academic robes so as not to stumble over them.

THE SCAVENGER HUNT FOR TRUTH

LIST: These are some of the things we are searching for:

1. A fig leaf from the Garden of Eden.
2. A street map from Atlantis.
3. Diogenes' Lantern.
4. A thread from the fabric of space.
5. The Holy Grail.
6. A stalactite from Plato's Cave.
7. An item bought from the Store of Knowledge.
8. A candle lit from the Light of Reason.
9. One of Demonsthenes' pebbles.
10. The chicken who crossed the road.
11. Something laudable from the Delphic Oracle.
12. Any one or more of the following:
    a. earth
    b. air
    c. fire
    d. water
13. The ear plugs won by God at The Big Bang.
14. A handful of muck from Heraclitus' River of Flux.
15. A photo of Godot (or Bardot.)
16. A juicy bit of gossip from the Tower of Babel.
17. Ichabod Crane's travel itinerary.
18. An unthinkable thought.
19. Nous.
20. A branch from the Tree of Knowledge.
21. Any one of a thousand angels found standing on the head of a pin.
22. Methuselah's Metamucil.
23. A spoke from Apollo's Chariot.
24. A bottle of sparkling water from the Spring of Life.
25. Manna from Heaven.

26. A nail bent by Nietsche's hammer.

27. A hair cut by Ockham's razor.

28. A lark from Noah's Ark.

29. The author's luggage last seen on the shuttle to New York.

30. Nirvana.

INSTRUCTIONS:

This project can be started at any time, preferably at one's leisure.
All things have to be sought after and found by yourself.
There is no time limit.
Start out by seeking truth in your own neighborhood, and places that
are familiar to you, but all other areas are open to rummaging as well.
Leave no stone unturned.
Except for the Store of Knowledge, merchandising centers are off limits.

SEND RESULTS TO:
Peter Payack
700 Huron Ave, Apt. 16J
Cambridge, MA 02138

BLOWING IN THE WIND, *part two*

I like the idea
of a Buddhist prayer flag

where the vibrations of the wind
blow goodwill and compassion
into the world

while I just sit
on my fat ass.

THE RESULT OF THE DIG

"So it finally turned out that after endless years of digging
and researching, the only bones found at the Olduvai
Gorge were those of fellow anthropologists, who
likewise were searching for earlier evolutionary specimens.
You had Neanderthals looking for Homo Erectus,
Homo Erectus excavating for Australopithecinus,
Australopithecinus probing for the early anthropoid apes,
who in turn sought out the first mammals. The earliest
thing they found was a tree shrew, and nobody knows
exactly what he might have been looking for, though
frankly by that time nobody gave a damn."

THE INSTITUTE FOR SCIENTIFIC
NON-RATIONAL THOUGHT

The recent hoopla surrounding the debate between the Creationists with their literal interpretation of Biblical Creation, and the Darwinists, who believe in the Theory of Evolution, has once again focused the world's intellectual eye not only on the nature of truth and what role it should play in our post-industrial society, but also who owns the copyright to it, not to mention the inevitable book and movie rights.

In an effort to settle this gnawing controversy, I have set up a research-oriented group, the Institute for Scientific Non-rational Thought. This institute, which prefers to be known by its acronym ISNT, will attempt to aid and abet the growing movement toward the illogical by formulating and articulating preposterous position papers for the various dogmatic disciplines of non-rational thought. These include, of course, the numerous occult sciences (astrology, numerology, creationism, the belief in a flat Earth, alchemy, pyramidology, etc.), along with other highly developed schools of sophisticated silliness that are deemed essential for survival in our confusing and morally degenerate world.

With this in mind, I thought *Absolute Truth* © 1982 would best be served if I delineated, not only for the first time in these pages, but a nywhere in print, the basic premises under which ISNT investigators work:

The Six Steps Of The Scientific Non-rational Method

1. Recognize a problem exists. If you don't readily recognize a problem, don't panic. Simply make one up! As a last resort, consult either an Ouija board or an astrologer.

2. Gather all the data you can find that either bears directly on the problem or simply looks good. Appearances are important especially when applying for grant monies.

3. Do not try, no matter how tempting, to sort out and discard non-essential aspects of the problem. This is definitely *passé,* if not downright boring. Instead, attempt to complicate matters with as many obscure absolutes, "givens," dogmatic truths, obnoxious axioms, and non-sequiturs as possible.

4. Postulate a hypothesis, a tentative (and tenuous) generalization. Make it as broad, ambiguous, and outrageous as possible. It is of utmost importance for you to form some sort mathematical relationship to your hypothesis so consult a Cabbalist. If you need assistance in making your supposition sound plausible, ask a politician to help you with jingoistic jargon. With any luck at all, your guess will be a good one!

5. With your hypothesis in hand, try to predict the results of an experiment of your making. Bolster your prediction with plenty of supporting passages from the Old Testament prophets. Have Faith it will work out.

6. If the experiment fails miserably, don't sweat it! Technically it isn't necessary for your hypothesis to hold up. The results can be exaggerated or, better yet, simply ignored. As long as you can cite Heisenberg's *Uncertainty Principle,* anything goes! Make reference to The Patience of Job while calling the doubter's Faith into question.

ONE CAUTIONARY NOTE:

Always be on the guard against new observations, ideas, or theories. Why let upstart evidence get in the way of a theory that has already been scrutinized by ISNT researchers and certified as *Absolute Truth* © 1982.

Of course, this is the ideal version of the scientific non-rational method. However, if times does not permit, rash judgments can be made without it.

This methodology of thought and action not only can be used to obscure and confuse findings of so-called scientists. It can also be utilized in everyday life whenever you are making outrageous statements, prejudicial remarks, and wild guesses or just speaking plain olde-fashioned foolishness.

SPACED (INSIDE) OUT

Are there Extraterrestrials out there?

Be more concerned with the strange being
that lives inside your head.

TACKLING & BEYOND

At football practice Little Justin, the smallest kid on our Mighty Mite team takes a hard hit from Seymah (The Tank) Burnett. Justin weighs just under 60 pounds, while The Tank is all of 80 pounds, and most of that is muscle. Surprisingly, Little Justin tackles the Tank, and takes him down hard. "Good coaching," I think, giving myself the proverbial pat on the back. While the Tank jumps to his feet, Little Justin struggles to his feet and tells me he saw stars. As the tackling drill goes on around us, I take him aside, and Justin confides that not only did he see stars, but "planets, moons, asteroids, comets, solar systems and even galaxies." I tell him we'll keep that little bit of information between ourselves, as I help him walk it off.

Wouldn't you know it, the next time Justin comes up to the line of scrimmage he has to face Seymah again! But Little Justin is a trooper. He put his head down and the two of them meet in a mighty crack of pads. As I help him to his feet Little Justin tells me, not only did he see stars but this time he saw the actual limits of the universe: pulsars, quasars, and even what he thought to be a black hole!

That was the last thing little Justin said before he vanished before my eyes.

Now, not only do I have to look for a new corner back, but I have to tell his mother what happened.

I tell you, facing the parents is the toughest part of coaching.

Peter Payack was the Head Coach of the Cambridge Pop Warner Mighty Mites who had a five year undefeated streak back in the 1990's.

THE LIGHT OF HUMAN REASON

When I mockingly named the light bulb I installed in the kitchen the "Light of Human Reason," I chuckled with my cleverness and insightful wit. But that was before I realized its quality as a beaming conversationalist. In no time at all, the light became my constant companion and confidant. For many long nights we held glowing discussions and illuminating debates on the necessity of the Punic Wars, the military strategy of Julius Caesar, the astronomy of Ptolemy, the poetry of Catullus, and the virtues of the Roman Empire in general. Then, as the light began to fade, in panic, we agonized over the empire's inherent weaknesses and imminent fall. Now, with the light flickering, I huddle under the table, ominously awaiting the invasion of the Goths; the onset of the Dark Ages.

Written in the 1500th
year since the fall of
the Empire

BLINDED BY THE SLIGHT
(Of The Light)

Look around you in the daytime.
What do you see?
There is no hint to the vastness
and ridiculous magnitude
of the universe.
All you see is land, houses,
people, cars etc.
No notion of the eternal and infinite.

But at night,
there is a hint there is more out there.....
And using our intelligence
we have taken many ludicrous leaps
to find out what lies
beyond this paltry planet.

NOW THE BON VIVANT

Genghis Khan,
the acknowledged world traveler
who devastated much of western Europe
    in the 13th century
is at it again!

Oh, won't that nasty
    Mongol conqueror
ever learn?

This time, however,
he is not leading
the internationally renowned death troupe
    "The Golden Horde"
but is gadding about the continent
    as a first class tourist
with all the necessities cared for:
    champagne breakfasts,
limos to extravaganzas
and even luncheons with luminaries.

"If only they had such excursions
    back in the Middle Ages,"
he bemoaned.

The only drawback now
is that Genghis has to shell out
    for the departure tax
at each European airport.
"Things weren't like that,"
    he confided to me rather demonically,
"when I ruled the world!"

UNRAVELING THE MUMMY MYSTERY

"D'yaknowhat?" Mike says when he wants to tell me something.
"D'yaknowhat?" he says it again as is his custom, making sure that he
has my full attention. Full fatherly attention, which means don't read,
don't watch TV, don't walk, don't look around, don't breathe. So, not
reading, not walking, not watching TV, not looking around, I gaze
directly into his eyes and say (and remember I'm doing this without
breathing), "What, son?" To which Mike responds with, "D'yaknowhat,
Peter?" And patiently I say, "What Mike?" because I love his little boy
voice, especially when it reaches a higher pitch tinged with the
excitement that another mystery of the world has been unraveled by his
four year old mind. No matter how many times in a day he says
"D'yaknowhat?" I love how he says it. It is music to my ears and
golden nectar to my soul. "D'yaknowhat mummies are, Peter? I saw
them in a book, and D'yaknowhat? They are dead people who've been
dead for thousands of years, and even though they don't have any cuts
they're wrapped up in bandages!" While I'm hugging him, he says,
"Do you want to see were I got cut today?" He then holds up the band
aid on his little finger with the enthusiasm of Champollion on
discovering the key to deciphering the Rosetta Stone.

THE CREATION OF THE UNIVERSE

In one sector of the galaxy,
it is taught that there once
was a god who indeed was responsible
for the creation of the cosmos
but was killed
when the mixture he was concocting
grew unstable and exploded.

This is what they term in their cosmogony,
(in a mocking way for the god's carelessness)
"The Big Bang."

The universe as we know it,
the myth goes on,
is constructed out of the debris
of that ill-fated experiment.*

*This is the basis for their claim:
"We Believe In The God, But Deny His Existence."

HERE COMES DA JUDGE

According to St. Augustine
   who I studied at Harvard
   of all places,
people can't judge people
only God
can judge people.

And since
I don't believe in God
   nobody
can judge me...

So go fuck yourself.

RAINBOW BRIDGES

An environmentally enlightened engineer decides
that all riverways, canyons, crevices, and valleys
are to be bridged by rainbows.

A rainbow bridge
is a more natural and aesthetic way
to connect two separate land masses.

This evanescent design was chosen
because of its imperviousness
to wind, storm, and flying creatures.

The lightweight and immaterial bridges
will be planned to hold seven lanes of traffic.
Red, orange, and yellow will be restricted
to high speed commercial vehicles.
Green, blue, and violet will be designated
for passenger cars.
Indigo will be reserved for pedestrians,
bicyclists, and runners.

Handrails and flashing lights will be added
to assure the safety
of those on foot.

It is hoped the faint glow of the roadway itself
will ease drivers' eyestrain.

Until engineers can perfect a practical
nighttime model,
the rainbow bridges will be operational
only on sunny days.

THE EVOLUTIONARY RACE

I run the beach
six miles in two hours,
pathetically slow,
but not bad for a sixty-five year old guy
with two knee replacements.

Then I pass a horseshoe crab
that has gone almost nowhere
in roughly half a billion years.

ILLUMINATING THE DARKNESS

Having devoted myself to endless years of abstract study of the abysmal blackness of the Dark Ages, I finally decided to so something pragmatic with all this accumulated knowledge. So I called an electrician who, even though he lacked any precise knowledge of the medieval world, agreed to turn off the electricity, dismantle the outlets, and adapt the existing fixtures to my proposed needs. It was in no time at all before he installed the first illuminated manuscript, *Confessions* by Augustine, into the lamp stand. I then placed a shade on top of it, cutting down the amount of glare and distributing the warm glow to all corners of the room. And some people say that scholarship is non-functional! I placed other manuscripts throughout the house, in the expected places. On the night tables in the bedroom I placed matching *Proofs of the Existence of God* by Anselm. (I've always prided myself on my interior decorating ability.) The rather ornate but not gaudy *Summa Theologica* was hung in the dining room above the table. It was a weighty work, so I had to help install it. On top of the refrigerator, where the lamp with the built-in clock used to be, I placed a copy of *A Book of Hours*. I was really pleased with my glowing achievements, until a few nights later when I tripped over myself, as the manuscript in the bathroom burnt out. Luckily, I had a vast library of lesser known and less brilliant manuscripts that I could use as night lights. I replaced the bathroom "bulb" with a loose page from a worm-eaten treatise by a discredited alchemist.

COSMIC COWBOYS

If,
like an endless cavalcade of cowboys
fading forever into the sunset,

    one-tenth of the universe
    has already been bushwhacked
    and swallowed by black holes,

Then,
black holes must be
the outlaws of outer space,

    relentlessly rustling matter
    corralling energy
    and lassoing light

across the astral plains
of the remote frontiers of space.

DARKNESS AT DAWN

Now that it is wintertime
with the days becoming alarmingly short
Peter Paul has taken to asking me, shyly,
with his eyes lowered
and his voice almost inaudible,

"Daddy, is it going to get dark, today?"

Bewildered, he asks me his question everyday.
Sometimes, right after waking,
I'll say, "Good morning, Babe.
How you doing?" And he'll say,
"Hi Dad." And then hesitantly adds,
as if he is asking me to reveal
one of the secrets of the universe,
"Daddy, is it going to get dark today?"
To this I answer,
"Yea, but not until later."
And then with a visible sigh of relief
he begins his day.

When he asks me this question
I feel a sinking sensation
because he is asking me about more than darkness,
about those imponderables in life
which he isn't sure how to handle:

From, "Why do I have to go to school?"
To, "When I grow up will I have to get married
and live in another house?"
Underlying all this,
is the lurking, most basic question,
(the question which begets all other questions)
"Daddy, will you grow old and die someday,
and leave me forever?"

When I answer this daily question,
about darkness at the break of dawn
I understand Peter Paul's
accepting, yet tentative, smile.

UNIVERSAL KISS-OFF

When she told him she "needed some space,"
Yves' first thought was to give her all the space she wanted.
Would the space between earth and the moon be enough?

Then he thought,
they had a long, close relationship,
maybe 250,000 miles wasn't sufficient!
So he figured he'd grant her wish
and give her all the space between Earth and Mars.
Now, we're talking 300 million miles here,
so maybe that would do.

Unfortunately they are planning a mission
to that faraway world, so maybe that
wouldn't work out either.
"Too close for comfort," he thought.

How about, he reasoned, just beyond
the edge of the solar system
to the Kuiper Belt where comets originate?
But that wasn't good enough either,
as some comets have cyclical periods
where they fly by earth.
Say, like Halley's comet,
which returns every 87 years.
He didn't like the idea
that she could return,
even that far in the future.

Finally, an idea flashed before his eyes
like a brilliant shooting star:

If she really wanted space,
he'd give her the whole universe:
The complete cold, cataclysmic, lifeless,
dark, barren, energy-suckin' black hole filled,
matter annihilating antimatter strewn,
dark energy infested, purposeless,
entropic doomed
universe.

SOULAR

A new radar detector
that has recently been invented
can not only detect rainbows

as was its original intention

but also has the unexpected
yet astonishing power
of seeing people's souls.

While meteorologists
and weather enthusiasts
are all aglow about this new
innovation,

blithely code named "Soular,"

civic and church
authorities are looking
leerily at this new invention.

Church Officials
are distressed about meteorologists
meddling in matters
previously the domain
of people of the cloth,

not to mention it being
somewhat unethical to have
lay people voyeuristically
gawking into a person's
soul.

The Surgeon General
has now also become involved
and recommended against
Government approval.
Her rationale:
The soul has never before
been considered
a bodily part
and is therefore beyond
their scope of investigation.

In addition,
The Civil Liberties Union
has intervened
and has asked for a court injunction
to put a stop
to the test trials of this new mechanism.

Under the Fourth Amendment
of the constitution
this is considered
an invasion of personal privacy.
The constitution holds it
illegal to search
a person's house,
and the body being a "temple"
makes it illegal
to peer into a person's
most vital essence.

WHY I BELIEVE IN DEATH
-A Brief Inquiry-

NOTE: This essay was written by Peter Payack in answer to a request by a friend, characteristic of the latter's morbid obsession with the subject.

The question of the existence of Death is at the same time both interesting and profound. Long before history was recorded, over 10,000 years ago, we can find evidence of early people's belief in Death. Red ochers and skeletons found in graves attest to this. However, in this essay, we are not concerned with prehistoric humanity's superstitious and ill-formed beliefs, but more significantly with historical people's view.

Today scholars, freethinkers, and neurotics alike agree that there are three credible arguments which lend proof to the existence of Death.

(1)

The first offers ontological proof, by asserting that the fact that the human mind can conceive of an infinite period of non-existence, necessarily means that such a state exists. This was first argued by St. Anselm (1033-1109), and he's been dead now for over 900 years. Q.E.D.

(2)

The second argument is that of Natural Law. This is grounded on the fact that one sees a majestic design of dissolution everywhere in the natural world: exploding galaxies, black holes, and soil erosion along the New Jersey shoreline. Everything in the world is falling apart in a uniform fashion, and (the argument continues) Death is responsible for all this. The major stumbling block with this polemic is in viewing Death in too anthropomorphic a fashion.

(3)

The third, and one of the most comprehensible, is that of the Last Result. Here it is maintained that everything in the universe is the result of something else, and as one goes down the chain of results further and further one comes finally to the Last Result, and you give that result the name Death.

Summary

These then are the major arguments for the existence of Death. It should be remembered though, that Death is a metaphysical entity which goes beyond the bounds of human intelligence. For this reason one should not be intimidated if s/he finds these arguments hard to follow. To millions around the world, Death is not a thing which has to be proved but is humbly accepted as a matter of faith.

RUMBLINGS ON REINCARNATION

It is true
you might be re-incarnated,

but it will be after
billions of years,
after The Sun goes supernova
and your elements are blown apart,
dispersed and reassembled
in a new star system.

What type of creature
a few of your molecules
might become part of
if at all,
is completely up to random chance.

But you can be most assured
you will not have the incredible gift
of self-consciousness you now enjoy.

ARCHEOLOGICAL TRUTHS

Seeking light in dark places.

∞

MICROCOSMOS

Star-gazing through the wrong end of the telescope.

RELATIVES AT SUNDAY DINNER

As you might have guessed, our peaceful Sunday dinner turned into a veritable verbal fistfight over the discussion of the relative size of the solar system. My brother Paul started it all.

"If the sun is the size of this orange," he said while grabbing a half-peeled navel orange out of my hands and dramatically placing it in the center of the table, "then the Earth would be the size of a grain of salt, circling the orange at thirty feet!" He next unscrewed the top off an antique salt shaker (much to my mother's dismay) and poured the contents into a little white pile. Then as smug as could be, he most carefully (in contrast to the barbaric way he previously dumped the salt) picked up a single crystal and ran to the far corner of the living room, a good 30 feet away.

Not one to be outdone, my older sister Bonnie seized a single olive, stuffed it into her mouth (quite disgustingly so, I might add), and spit out the pit at the same time she was spitting out the following words: "Likewise the planet Jupiter, which is eleven times larger than the earth, would be the size of an olive pit about one block away," Then she boogied out the front door with her olive pit, dancing and carrying on like one possessed by an ingenious idea, until she theatrically placed the pit under a telephone pole, a good 200 feet away.

Quite naturally we all got up from the dinner table and were standing at the door to watch her, when in a moment of inspiration, I snuck back to the table, grabbed a cherry, and scampered out the door. While chewing it I yelled back to my sister as I passed her, "And in much the same way Saturn, being a little smaller than Jupiter, would be a cherry pit a block farther down the street." As I streaked by her she stuck out her foot and tried to trip me, but I eluded her with an old halfback move.

Thinking we had proved our respective points, we once again (at my mother's persistent urging) reassembled at the table to finish our dessert. In the middle of eating our homemade Italian pastries, we were all seized with violent fits of sneezing when we noticed my younger sister Chrissy was in the process of emptying the pepper shaker. Before we could stop her she grabbed a single fleck with the tweezers she had been concealing, and pronounced, "By extension, the planet Pluto would be another ten blocks down the road or almost halfway to the train station." Then she bolted from the table like a young colt, and galloped out the door. Being a jogger, she made it back fairly quickly, as we were all finishing the last of the coffee.

As the evening wore on, we moved into the living room where things finally settled down to the normal family chatter. But my brother, who hours earlier had started it all, was uncharacteristically quiet. Not knowing when to leave well enough alone, he broke out of his reverie and ventured, "You know, I was doing some calculating, and on the same scale our galaxy would be a virtual citrus grove of more than one hundred billion oranges, tangerines, and grapefruit." As he said this he was juggling these fruit high above his head, much to my mother's horror. Then he serenely added, "And the nearest star would be Alpha Centauri, another orange, almost thirteen hundred miles away!"

Well, that was enough for my usually reticent father, who exploded like a volcano and ordered us to get into the family car. We all sat there in interstellar silence as he drove us to the train station. Upon arrival, he proceeded to the counter and came back smirking with four tickets. These he handed to us along with a parting paternal pat. He boarded us on the next train, which was just pulling out—destination: Alpha Centauri (Cleveland).

COSMOGONY

At one point the universe came into being.
The causality is still a mystery;
we can surmise a number of possible scenarios:

A child could have kicked a can a number of times,
    say, ten in a row without missing.
But on the eleventh try
    she misses and falls down.
And at that moment the galaxies are born.

A book could have been opened
    and then shut abruptly.
Conceivably, the reader was offended by a sentence
as it was perceived to be insulting to the intelligence;
or maybe he was disappointed
    in a phrase, a word, or a punctuation mark.
In any case, the book was shut abruptly,
and at that moment the cosmic dust
    from which the stars aggregate,
materialized.

Or, perhaps an older woman could have shed
a tear for a friend long dead.
And the tear could have fallen into an infinite abyss,
    picking up not only speed
but potential for being,
and grew to possess all the matter of eternity,
and time of infinity.

I am not convinced which of these actions
    if any, was the cause
for the reification of reality.

Conversely, one day,
reality might just as suddenly
    flash out of existence.
A possible impetus for this might simply be
reading the last line of a poem.

This poem.

"Sic Itur Ad Astra"

–Virgil, Aeneid, Book IX, Line 642

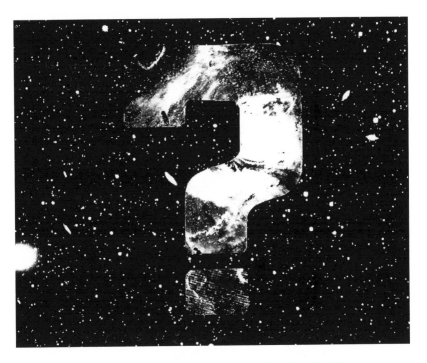

"Cosmic Question Mark," original collage by Peter Payack, 1981

ABOUT PETER PAYACK

Peter Payack is the First Poet Populist of Cambridge, Massachusetts. He is long renowned for putting poetry in public spaces and has done so as a commissioned artist at MIT's International Sky Art Conferences (Delphi, Greece), The Harvard 350th Anniversary celebration, the New York Avant Garde Festival and Boston's First Night.

His first foray into making poetry public was his innovation Phone-a-Poem, The Cambridge/Boston Poetry Hotline (1976-2001). This achievement has now been archived at the Woodberry Poetry Room at Harvard's Lamont Library. The Phone-a-Poem collection includes records, correspondence, ephemera, audiocassette tapes, clippings, personal papers and realia of Peter Payack, the founder. The collection has now been digitalized to hear such poets as Allen Ginsberg, Jane Kenyon and James Tate. He collaborated with Roland Pease over the years on this project.

Payack has published over 2,000 poems, stories, photos and articles including multiple appearances in *The Paris Review, Rolling Stone, The New York Times, The Cornell Review, Asimov's Science Fiction Magazines, Creative Computing, Amazing SF Stories* and *The Boston Globe*.

The poem, "The Migration of Darkness," won the 1980 Rhysling Award for the Best Poem in Science Fiction, and was named the number one poem that unites art and science by Quirk Press. The London Based *TES*, (*Times Educational Supplement*) uses the poem as Chapter 15, in its "What is Science Fiction?" web based course. The poem is also one of four featured in the MasterClass "How To Write Specuative Poetry" article.

Payack is one of handful of poets who has published in *Asimov's Science Fiction Magazine* for six decades starting in 1979.

His work has been anthologized extensively including pieces in *The Paris Review Anthology,* (Norton), *Knowing & Writing, New Perspectives on Classical Questions,* (Harper Collins), *Astronomy, from the Earth to the Universe* (Saunders College Publishing), *The Poets' Encyclopedia* (Unmuzzled Ox), *The Alchemy of Stars* (SFPA), and *Envisioning Other Worlds,* (Cornelson, Berlin).

He has 20 books and chapbooks, including *No Free Will in Tomatoes* and *Blanket Knowledge* from Zoland Books, and *The Book of Conceptual Anarchy, Vol. 1* from Assembly Line Studios.

Peter is the inventor of The Stonehenge Watch™, an infinitesimal replica of the megaliths at Stonehenge inside of an old-fashioned pocket watch, which can be used as a shadow clock to tell time, mark the seasons and predict eclipses. The Stonehenge Watch™ has been featured at The International Sky Art Conference at MIT, on BBC-TV, in *Astronomy Magazine,* and was named the official "eclipse predictor" for the Great American Solar Eclipse of 2017 by the noted astronomer, Jay Pasachoff, in *The American Journal of Physics.*

Payack's Poem, "No Free Will in Tomatoes" has been sandblasted into the brick floor of the Davis Square Subway Station (Boston's Red Line) since 1984. Peter was featured on the PBS Children's show *ARTHUR,* episode 1308, "Fernlets for Fern," and is pictured in *US Magazine* with his "Poetry Mobile."

Payack was awarded the 2010 Haskell Award for Distinguished Teaching at University of Massachusetts Lowell and was awarded a Commendation from the State of Massachusetts for his "Outstanding Contribution in Bringing Arts to The Commonwealth."

Payack has coached The Cambridge Rindge & Latin School Varsity wrestling team for the 25 years, and has run 100,000 miles including 23 Marathons.

You can read more about Peter at *www.peterpayack.com.*